HEIDI HECKELBECK
Has a Secret

HEIDI HECKELBECK
Casts a Spell

HEIDI HECKELBECK
and the Cookie Contest

By Wanda Coven
Illustrated by Priscilla Burris

LITTLE SIMON
New York   London   Toronto   Syney   New Delhi

This book is a work of fiction. Any references to historical events, real people, or real places are used fictitiously. Other names, characters, places, and events are products of the author's imagination, and any resemblance to actual events or places or persons, living or dead, is entirely coincidental.

LITTLE SIMON
An imprint of Simon & Schuster Children's Publishing Division
1230 Avenue of the Americas, New York, New York 10020
Copyright © 2012 by Simon & Schuster, Inc. This Little Simon bind-up edition 2014.
All rights reserved, including the right of reproduction in whole or in part in any form.
LITTLE SIMON is a registered trademark of Simon & Schuster, Inc., and associated colophon is a trademark of Simon & Schuster, Inc.
For information about special discounts for bulk purchases, please contact Simon & Schuster Special Sales at 1-866-506-1949
or business@simonandschuster.com.
Manufactured in the United States of America 0814 MTN
10 9 8 7 6 5 4 3 2
ISBN 978-1-4814-2771-5

CONTENTS

#1: HEiDi HECKELBECK
HAS A SECRET   5

#2: HEiDi HECKELBECK
CASTS A SPELL   129

#3: HEiDi HECKELBECK
AND THE
COOKIE CONTEST   253

HEIDI HECKELBECK
Has a Secret

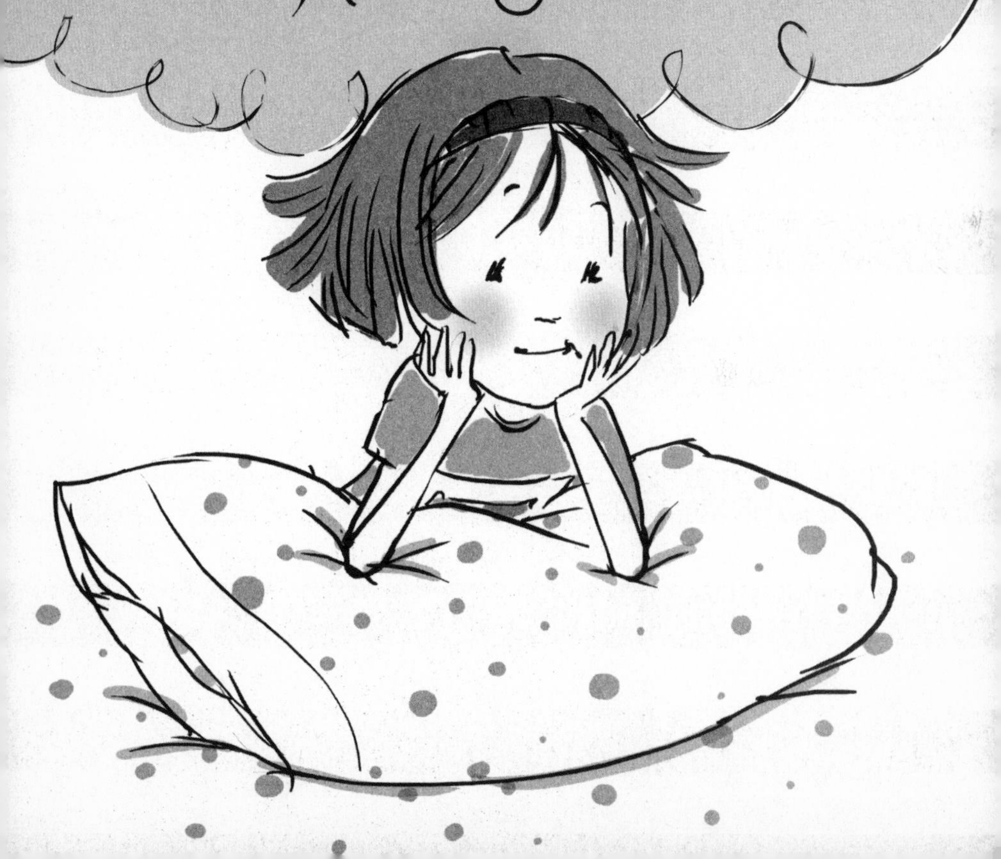

CONTENTS

Chapter 1: GROUCHY 9

Chapter 2: DOUBLE GROUCHY 25

Chapter 3: HELLO. MEANiE 33

Chapter 4: MEEP! MEEP! 45

Chapter 5: A NEW FRiEND 53

Chapter 6: BIG TROUBLE 63

Chapter 7: DRAMA QUEENS 77

Chapter 8: FOUR ANSWERS 93

Chapter 9: ZiNG! 99

Chapter 10: SMELL-A-NIE 109

Chapter 11: THE SECRET! 119

GROUCHY

Heidi Heckelbeck woke up in the Kingdom of Gloom.

Grouchy Land.

Grumpsville, USA.

Heidi felt like the princess of Crankypants. Because not only was it the first day of school—it was her first day of school EVER.

Heidi had never been to school before. She had always had school at home with her five-year-old brother, Henry. Mom had been their teacher. But starting today Heidi Heckelbeck would be a brand-new second grader at Brewster Elementary.

Mom popped her head into Heidi's room. "Time to get up!" she sang.

"Merg!" growled Heidi.

She flumped her pillow on top of her face. A million questions swirled in her head. What if the teacher was mean? What if she couldn't find her way to the bathroom? What if she sat next to a boy who picked his nose?

Heidi dragged herself out of bed and got dressed. She put on her black jean skirt with her kitty cat top. Then she wiggled into her black-and-white-striped tights and black sneakers. Not even her favorite outfit made her feel cheery. She plodded downstairs.

Mom placed a happy-face pancake in front of Heidi. It had blueberry eyes, a mouth of raspberries, and sausage eyebrows.

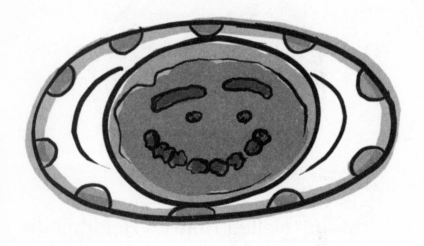

Heidi stuck out her tongue at her pancake.

"It's still smiling," said Henry.

Heidi used her fork to move the food around.

"Not anymore," said Heidi.

"Mom!" yelled Henry. "Heidi made a mad-face pancake!"

Heidi rolled her eyes.

"You know what?" said Henry as he dipped a sausage in syrup. "You

should wear pink. Pink looks friendly."

"Pretty in pink!" added Mom with a wink.

"Wait, what's wrong with the way I look?" said Heidi.

"Uh . . . nothing, really," said Henry.

"It's just that your outfit kind of looks like a Halloween costume. What if you spook the other kids on your first day of school?"

"Har-dee-har-har," said Heidi. But Henry's comment kind of bugged her.

Heidi's dad walked into the kitchen as he fixed his tie.

"Zip-a-dee-doo-dah, zip-a-dee-ay!" he sang. He stopped when he saw Heidi's unhappy face. She was not in a Disneyland mood.

"What's the matter, pumpkin?" asked Dad.

"Nothing," said Heidi. "I just don't want to go to school—EVER. That's all."

Henry dropped his fork.

"Never, ever?" asked Henry. "That means you won't get to have a class pet! Or your own personal desk! Or fire drills."

"Who cares?" said Heidi.

Dad sat down next to Heidi.

"All is well," said Dad. "And all will be well at school too."

"But I want to have school at home with Mom," said Heidi.

"We had a lot of fun," said Mom, "but now it's time to learn from teachers and books at school."

"I can teach myself," said Heidi. "Besides, I like *my* book better."

Mom raised her eyebrows.

"School needs you, Heidi," said Dad. "You're clever and kind."

"And kind of cuckoo," added Henry.

"Trust me," said Dad. "I know you're going to love school. And when you get home, you can be the first to test my brand-new fruit cola formula. I'm thinking of calling it Cherry Zing."

Mr. Heckelbeck worked at a soda pop company called The FIZZ. Heidi loved to try his secret formulas.

Sometimes Heidi came up with her own formulas and shared them with her dad. Tasting a new fruit cola did sound a tiny bit fun.

Mom jingled her car keys. "Time to go," she said cheerfully.

Heidi groaned and slid off of her chair. She put on her black jean jacket and backpack. Then she said her good-byes: "Good-bye, tree fort classroom! Good-bye, backyard cafeteria!"

"You forgot something," said Henry.

"What?" asked Heidi.

"HELLO, SCHOOL!"

And off they went.

Chapter 2

DOUBLE GROUCHY

Heidi wrote her favorite growly word on the foggy car window. *Merg!* She wished the drive to school would never end. She didn't want to learn double-digit addition. She did not feel like making new friends. Heidi squished an old Goldfish cracker into the crumb-filled floor mat. *Crunch*.

Mom parked in the Visitors Only parking spot.

"We're here!" she sang.

Heidi stared at the large brick building. Brewster Elementary looked like a dungeon. Why did it look so creepy? And why did it feel like she had eaten cotton balls for breakfast? And how come the car door felt so heavy?

"Hurry up!" said Henry.

He bounded up the steps and dashed through the door.

Heidi felt like she was wearing Frankenstein shoes. She clumped up the stairs. Mom followed.

The principal, Mr. Pennypacker, greeted them in the main office. He had a tuft of brown hair on either side of his head and no hair in the middle. Heidi thought his hairdo looked like earmuffs.

"I'll take Heidi to second grade," he said. "And my assistant, Mrs. Crosby, will take Henry to kindergarten."

Henry was so lucky. He only had to stay a half day. Heidi thought a half day sounded easy.

"Can I take the bus home, Mom?" begged Henry. "Can I? Can I?"

"Sure," said Mom. "And what about you, Heidi?"

"I want to be picked up."

Mom nodded. Then she gave Heidi and Henry a squeeze and slipped out the door.

Chapter 3

HELLO, MEANIE

Heidi followed Principal Pennypacker down the hall. It smelled like pencils and floor wax.

"You're going to love Brewster Elementary," said the principal.

I doubt it, thought Heidi.

They passed a winter wonderland

mural. It showed penguins sledding, snowboarding, and throwing snow-balls. Heidi thought it looked dumb.

"Do you like sports?" asked Principal Pennypacker.

"Nope," said Heidi.

"How about art?"

"Not really."

"Reading?"

"Kind of."

"What do you like to read?" he asked.

"My special book," said Heidi. "But I forget the name."

"Oh," said the principal.

When Heidi arrived at her classroom, her teacher came to the door.

"Oh, you must be Heidi," she said. "Welcome!"

Heidi studied the room. She saw a fish tank, a bulletin board about

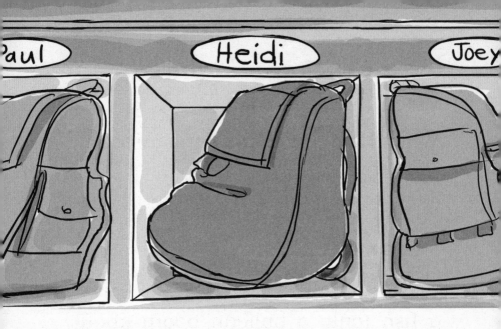

Dr. Martin Luther King Jr., and a reading corner with beanbag chairs.

"I'm Mrs. Wellington," she said. "But everyone calls me Mrs. Welli for short."

Mrs. Welli showed Heidi her cubby and her desk. The cubby had chipped red paint and a sticker with her name on it. Heidi pulled out her pencil case and notebook and stuffed her backpack into the cubby. She hung her jean jacket on a hook.

Then Heidi sat down at her desk. The lid squeaked when she opened it. The legs rocked when she leaned on

it. The only good thing about it was the shiny name tag on top. It had a number line, a hundreds chart, and the alphabet. Heidi scooched in her chair.

Mrs. Welli introduced Heidi to the class.

"Wel-come, Hei-di," they all said together.

Someone tapped a pencil.

Heidi looked.

It was a blond-haired girl in a purple ruffly skirt and a polka-dot top.

The girl scrunched her face at Heidi. Then she raised her hand.

"Yes, Melanie?" asked Mrs. Welli.

"Something's smelly, Mrs. Welli," she said with a pinched nose.

The class giggled.

Mrs. Welli clapped her hands. "That's enough, Melanie," she said.

Melanie smiled sweetly. Then she turned and made another mean face at Heidi.

Heidi looked the other way. *Why is this girl being so mean to me?* she wondered. Heidi sniffed her sleeve. *Do I really smell?*

Suddenly another girl, who was two rows up, turned around and looked at Heidi. Heidi braced herself for another prickly glare.

But this time she got a warm, fuzzy smile.

Chapter 4

MEEP!
MEEP!

One fuzzy smile did not fix a whole bunch of merg. Heidi sat at her desk and wondered, *Can an eight-year-old drop out of school?* While Heidi thought, she doodled an alien in her new enchanted forest notebook. She drew a thought bubble over her alien's head. *Meep! Meep! Get me off this creepy planet!* thought Heidi.

As she doodled, the teacher wrote homophones on the board. Heidi already knew about homophones. They were words that sounded the same but were spelled differently or had different meanings.

"Okay," said Mrs. Welli to the class. "Pick two sets of homophones and write a sentence for each one. Those of you who would like to share may raise your hand when you're ready."

Heidi looked at the words on the board. She picked two and wrote:

School is a big, fat bore.
Melanie is a mean, nasty boar.

I have a KNOT in my stomach.
I am not coming back to school.

Heidi looked up when she was done. The girl who had smiled at her had her hand up. Mrs. Welli called on her.

"You may come to the front of the classroom, Lucy."

Lucy walked up to the board.

"My words are 'holy' and 'holey,'" said Lucy. "And 'bare' and 'bear.'"

The chalk squeaked as she wrote. Lucy walked back to her desk when she was done. Then Mrs. Welli read Lucy's sentences out loud and under-lined each homophone:

<u>Holy</u> Toledo!
I have <u>holey</u> socks!

A <u>bear</u> ate our picnic.
My brother ran down
the street <u>bare</u> naked.

The class cracked up the whole time.

"Good work, Lucy!" said Mrs. Welli. Heidi thought Lucy's sentences were pretty good too, but that did not change Heidi's funky mood. She covered her own sentences with her arm so no one would see.

After language arts, Heidi sat through social studies and math. In math, they worked on fact families. *Bo-ring,* thought Heidi. Mom had already taught that at home. Heidi made up her own fact family, only instead of numbers she used words:

Heidi + School = Yuck

Yuck - Heidi = School

Yuck - School = Heidi

Her fact family kind of worked, she thought. At least it had helped her get all the way to lunch. *Just a few more hours and I can go home*, thought Heidi.

Chapter 5

A NEW FRiEND

Lunch.

Ugh.

Heidi had never had lunch in a cafeteria before. She didn't know anybody. She would have to sit all by herself. Double ugh. She grabbed her lunch from her cubby and followed the kids down the hall. Someone shouted her name.

"Heidi! Heidi!"

It was Henry. He waved like crazy from the school bus line.

Heidi gave Henry a *shhhh* face.

Henry ignored her.

"Isn't school FUN?" he said excitedly. "We got to do musical movement and paint decorations for the school play!"

Heidi gave Henry a halfhearted high five and kept walking. He was so happy, it was weird.

The lunchroom smelled like stinky soup. Heidi found an empty table and

sat down on a cold plastic seat. She pulled out her peanut-butter-and-grape-jelly sandwich and chocolate chip cookie. A note was taped to her sandwich. It read:

The note from Mom made Heidi miss home even more. Not even her favorite sandwich tasted right.

"May I sit here?" a girl asked.

It was Lucy. The girl who smiled and wrote funny sentences. Heidi nodded her head up and down.

"My name is Lucy Lancaster," she said.

Heidi nodded again.

"How do you like school so far?" Lucy asked.

Heidi looked at the table.

"That's okay," said Lucy. "It'll get better. So guess what?"

"What?" asked Heidi.

"We have play practice today. Our grade is doing *The Wizard of Oz.*"

Gulp. Heidi did not like the sound of a play. The last thing she wanted was to be in the spotlight.

"I'm going to be Auntie Em plus a Munchkin," Lucy went on. "Pretty cool, right?"

"I guess," said Heidi.

Lucy told Heidi who got the best parts.

Soon the bell rang.

"Want to play at recess?" asked Lucy.

Heidi thought that sounded kind of okay. "Sure," she said.

Wow, now Heidi the Alien had a friend.

Meep! Meep!

Chapter 6

BIG TROUBLE

"This is the art room," said Lucy. "Isn't it great?"

Heidi looked around. The art room looked like a children's museum. The walls had paintings of owls and lady-bugs and rocket ships and monsters. Mobiles dangled from the ceiling.

Clay creatures lined the shelves.

"See that bird's nest mobile?" said Lucy. She pointed at the ceiling. "That's mine. It has real birds' eggs inside of it."

Melanie overheard Lucy talking.

"That's right," said Melanie. "Real stinky eggs." She gave Lucy and Heidi a scrunchy face and turned away.

Lucy rolled her eyes. "As I was saying," she said, "you're going to love art."

Heidi stunk at art. She could barely draw a stick figure. She had never worked with clay or made a mobile.

And most of all she did not want to do art anywhere near Melanie. Heidi sat down at a table in the corner. Lucy sat next to her. At each place was a piece of white construction paper and a foam plate with dabs of colored paint. A coffee can full of paintbrushes sat at the middle of the table with two cups of water to dip brushes.

"Smocks on, everyone! Chop-chop!"

said the art teacher as he clapped.

"That's Mr. Doodlebee," whispered Lucy. "He's really nice."

Mr. Doodlebee had a long brown ponytail. He wore a T-shirt with a

swirly design on it, paint-speckled jeans, and red high-tops. Heidi thought he looked like a skateboarder.

"Today we're going to paint self-portraits," said the teacher. "Let's get started. I'll come around to help."

Heidi stared at her paper. *Should I draw my alien self or my regular self?* she wondered. *Is there really any difference?* She dabbed a brush in pale pink paint and drew an oval face. She painted blue eyes with light brown eyelashes. She drew a pointy little nose and a purple line for a mouth. Then she painted strands of red hair.

The teacher came to the table and watched as Heidi painted.

"Nice work," said the teacher. "You must be Heidi. I'm Mr. Doodlebee."

Heidi kept painting.

"I'm here if you need help," said Mr. Doodlebee, and he moved on to another table.

What Heidi really needed was some brown paint to mix in with the red. She got up and went to the paint station. She pumped a glop of brown

paint from a jar. But when she came back, Melanie was at her place. She had painted a zigzag mouth on Heidi's picture.

"Stop it!" said Heidi.

"What's wrong?" asked Melanie. "I just made your picture look more like you."

Heidi picked up her paintbrush and wiped it across Melanie's smock.

Melanie shrieked and swiped her paintbrush at Heidi. But Melanie missed because Mr. Doodlebee had grabbed her arm in midair.

"Come with me," said Mr. Doodlebee, and he marched Melanie straight to the principal's office.

Heidi crumpled up her self-portrait and dropped it on the table. Melanie Maplethorpe had to be the meanest girl on planet Earth. She felt a tear roll down her cheek. She wiped her eyes with the back of her arm. She could hear kids whispering things.

"Are you okay?" asked Lucy.

"No," said Heidi. "I'm not okay. I want to go home!"

Tears spilled from Heidi's eyes.

When Mr. Doodlebee returned to the classroom, he asked Heidi to come into his office. He gave her tissues and told her that everything would be okay. Heidi felt too embarrassed to say anything. She stayed in his office until the end of art.

Then there was a knock on the door. It was Lucy.

"Hey, Heidi," she said. "I've got good news."

"What?" asked Heidi.

"Melanie got in BIG trouble."

Chapter 7

DRAMA QUEENS

Big mouth.

Big liar.

Big meanie.

"That Melanie is nothing but BIG trouble," said Heidi.

Heidi and Lucy laughed as they walked to play practice. Heidi hadn't

laughed all day. It felt really good.

In the auditorium a round lady with curly orange hair was playing the piano. Heidi recognized the song. It was "Somewhere over the Rainbow."

The girls walked onto the stage and sat at a table. Behind them was a set of the Yellow Brick Road with the Emerald City in the distance. When everyone was seated, the lady stopped playing. Her heels clickety-clacked up the stairs and onto the stage.

"Hello, boys and girls!" said the teacher. "I have your scripts today!" She waved an emerald green script back and forth so everyone could see.

"Melanie and Stanley, please pass these out."

The teacher handed them each a stack of scripts.

A script landed in front of each
student.

Melanie paused when she got to Heidi.

"Mrs. Noddywonks?" said Melanie sweetly. "Does the new girl get one too?"

"Yes, dear. Everybody should get one," said Mrs. Noddywonks.

Melanie dropped a script in front of Heidi. It landed with a thud. Heidi kept her eyes on the table. Then Mrs. Noddywonks called her name.

"Heidi?" she said as she put on her glasses and looked for Heidi. "Heidi Heckelbeck? Did I pronounce your last name correctly?"

Heidi nodded.

"Hello, honey," said Mrs. Noddy-wonks. "Welcome to the wonderful land of Oz! Our play has already been cast, but don't worry, we'll find something fun for you to do."

Phew! thought Heidi. She didn't

have to worry about being in the play. But wait. What was going on? Meanie Melanie was whispering something to Mrs. Noddywonks.

Mrs. Noddywonks nodded and looked at Heidi.

"I have wonderful news, Heidi!" Mrs. Noddywonks said excitedly. "Melanie has found a part for you in the play!"

Heidi's hair stuck straight out of her head—or at least it felt that way. She did not want a part in the play. She did not want to be a flying monkey. She did not want to be a tin girl, a cowardly lion, a scarecrow, or anything else.

"No, thank you, Mrs. Noddywonks," said Heidi. "I would rather *not* be in the play."

"I know how you feel," said Mrs. Noddywonks. "Melanie told me all about it."

"All about what?" asked Heidi.

"About how you feel left out."

"But I want to be left out," said Heidi.

"Hogwash!" said Mrs. Noddywonks.

"Please tell Heidi your idea, Melanie."

Melanie nodded and smiled.

"As Heidi's new friend," began Melanie, "I am happy to say that she will play the role of a scary apple tree in our school play."

"You know the trees I'm talking about," she went on. "The ones in the Haunted Forest."

Everyone looked at Heidi.

She wanted to throw her script at Melanie.

Lucy squished Heidi's foot under the table. "It'll be okay," she whispered.

"Well, then, it's all settled," said Mrs. Noddywonks. She put on her glasses. "Let's practice pages one through sixteen."

Heidi wanted to scream. Melanie thought she was so BIG. She acted like she owned the second-grade. There was only ONE role for that girl: the Wicked Witch. She wouldn't even need to act! But Melanie hadn't gotten the part of the witch. She had gotten Dorothy! Heidi folded her arms.

Talk about UNFAIR. But then Heidi realized something. If Heidi played a scary apple tree and Melanie played Dorothy, then that could mean only one thing. Heidi would get to throw apples at Melanie.

Now, THAT sounded like fun.

Chapter 8

FOUR ANSWERS

Somehow Heidi lived through an entire day of school. But for her, it felt like an entire *year* of school. She wanted a medal, a hug, and a big bowl of peppermint ice cream with hot fudge sauce. Instead, when Mom picked her up, she got to sit next to Henry, who had his finger in his nose.

"That's so gross," said Heidi.

"What?" said Henry. "Boogers taste great."

"Double gross," said Heidi.

"Did you miss me?" said Henry.

"No," said Heidi.

"Well, I missed you all afternoon," said Henry. "It's boring without you."

"You're weird," said Heidi. "But thanks, bud."

Mom smiled in the rearview mirror.

"So," said Mom, "how was your first day of school?"

Now *that* was a juicy question. Heidi thought of four answers. She could:

1. remain silent

2. scream without
stopping

3. explode

4. tell it like it was

Heidi chose answer number four.

"I hated being new," said Heidi. "I felt like an alien all day."

"That's so cool!" said Henry. "What planet are you from?"

"Planet I-Hate-School," said Heidi.

"Never heard of it," said Henry.

"It's awful," said Heidi. "It has a mean-girl leader named Melanie."

"Does she smell?" said Henry. "Because if she smells, you could call her Princess Smell-a-nie."

"Worse," said Heidi. "She said that *I* smell!"

"Wow," said Henry. "She must have a smelly problem."

"Enough smelly talk," said Mom. "I'm sure Melanie didn't mean it."

Of course she meant it, thought Heidi. The name Princess Smell-a-nie was perfect. All Melanie needed was a stinky crown on top of her head.

Chapter 9

ZING!

When Heidi got home, Dad was in the kitchen. He had two plastic bottles filled with dark liquid on the table. One was labeled SAMPLE NUMBER 1, and the other was labeled SAMPLE NUMBER 2. There was also a bottle of water and a stack of mini paper cups.

"She's home! My big school girl

is home!" said Dad. Dad gave Heidi a great big squeeze. She managed a small smile.

"Are you ready?" asked Dad.

"Ready," said Heidi.

Dad had on his white lab coat. He set out two cups and then rubbed his hands together for the big moment.

"Welcome to the Heckelbeck Taste-Testing Laboratory," he said. "As you can see, we have two mystery drinks to choose from today. Please sample one, followed by a glass of water. Then sample the second one. Do not. I repeat. *Do not* make yummy faces *or* yucky faces during the taste test. We

do not want to sway the other tasters."

Dad poured a cup of dark fizzy liquid and a cup of water. He placed both of them in front of Heidi.

"My trusty assistant, Heidi, will go first," said Dad. "Remember, *no* faces!"

Heidi took a sip of the soda. She felt the tingle of the bubbles on her tongue. It had a nice cherry flavor to

it. She set down the cup and sipped some water.

"Now for sample number two," said Dad. He poured the second mystery liquid and handed it to Heidi.

Heidi slowly sipped it. *Wow-wee!* she thought, trying not to let the wow-wee show in her face. This soda had a super-tingly, super-zingy cherry flavor. She set down the cup and sipped some water. Then Mom and Henry took their turns.

"Okay, let's hear from taste-tester number one," said Dad.

"I choose sample number two," said Heidi.

"Taste-tester number two?" asked Dad.

"I pick number two also," said Henry.

"Taste-tester number three?"

"Number two," said Mom.

Dad pumped his fists in the air.

"I'm happy to say that the taste test was a success!" said Dad. "Cherry Zing is the winner!"

Dad looked so happy. He worked so hard on his soda formulas. He wanted

them to be the best. Heidi was very
proud of him.

"Thanks for your help, guys," said Dad. "So, Heidi, how was your first day of school?"

Oh no, thought Heidi. *Not THAT again*. She felt the fun drain right out of her body. *Droooooop*.

"Going to school was absolutely, positively the worst thing I've ever done in my life," said Heidi.

"Worse than fabric shopping with your mother?" asked Dad.

"Way worse," said Heidi. "I felt like a complete doofus all day. I just don't fit in at school."

All the yucky feelings of the day bubbled up all over again. Heidi felt awful. She ran upstairs to her room and slammed the door.

Chapter 10

SMELL-A-NiE

Heidi kicked off her shoes and flopped onto her bed. She buried her face in her pillow. Maybe she could stay in bed the rest of her life. That sounded perfect.

Heidi heard the doorknob turn. It was Mom. She came in and sat down on the bed beside Heidi.

"Pretty yucky day, huh?" said Mom.

"Yup," said Heidi in a muffled-pillow voice.

"I know how you feel," said Mom. "It happened to me too."

Heidi rolled over and looked at her mother.

"It did?" questioned Heidi. "When?"

"In grade school," said Mom. "Some of the girls in my class thought I was—you know—different."

"Well, we *are* different," said Heidi. "So, what did you do?"

"I made two really good friends,

and then the mean girls didn't bug me as much."

Heidi sighed.

"You know what I wish?" said Heidi. "I wish I could just be my real self. Why can't I just be a—"

Before Heidi could finish, Henry burst into the room. He had on Mom's high heels and a pair of glasses perched on the end of his nose. He had an open book in his hand.

"Wanna play school?" asked Henry. "We can both be the teachers and my stuffed animals can be the students."

"Not in the mood," said Heidi.

"But I already set up all the stuffed animals on chairs and everything," said Henry. "They're ready to learn!"

"Maybe later," said Heidi.

"Why? Are you still upset about that Smell-a-nie girl?" asked Henry.

"Pretty much," said Heidi.

"Well, I have an idea," said Henry.

"Shoot," said Heidi.

"When Smell-a-nie talks to you, pretend that she has a pair of underwear on her head," said Henry. "Then she won't seem so scary."

"You are a total Froot Loop," said Heidi.

"Who knows? It might work," said Mom. "But one thing I can promise is that school will get better. Now, who's up for an after-school snack?"

"Cookies?" asked Henry.

"Why not?" said Mom.

Henry raced out the door.

Mom got up and looked at Heidi.

"Uh . . . I'll be down in a sec," said Heidi. A brilliant idea had just popped into her head.

"Okay," said Mom.

Chapter 11

THE SECRET!

Once Mom and Henry were gone, Heidi shut the door. Then she lay down on her stomach and pulled her keepsake box out from under her bed. It was bejeweled with rainbow gems and glitter. Heidi undid the silver latch and opened the box. She pulled out a golden medallion on a long

chain. In the middle of the medallion was the letter *W* woven into another *W*. Heidi slipped the medallion over her head. It hung all the way to her lap. She held it in one hand and studied it. Heidi traced the *W* with her finger. A big smile bloomed on her face. Her idea was beautiful. And

wicked. But before starting she would need a snack. She stuck the medallion back into the box and ran downstairs.

"Mom, can I have some cookies?" asked Heidi. "I need some energy to do my homework."

"Coming right up!" said Mom. She put two chocolate chip cookies on a plate.

"Does that mean you're going back to school?" asked Henry.

"Yup," said Heidi. "Your underwear trick was just what I needed."

"Really?" asked Henry.

"No," said Heidi.

Heidi ate her cookies, gave Mom a

big hug, and went back upstairs.

Mom almost dropped the milk jug.

"Whoa," said Mom to Henry. "What just happened here?"

Henry shrugged.

As soon as Heidi got back to her room, she pulled out her keepsake box again. This time she pulled out an old worn black leather book. The title on the cover read *Book of Spells*. She opened the book. The first page had a list of fancy signatures. Above the signatures it said *"The Witches of Westwick."* Heidi flipped through the pages. She stopped when she came

to the one that read: *"How to Make Someone Forget."*

"Perfect!" Heidi said to herself with a smile. "Let's see what happens when Princess Smell-a-nie forgets her lines in the play. . . ."

Heidi folded her arms.

One thing's for sure, thought Heidi. *I'm not going to forget who I am. I'm Heidi Heckelbeck, and I'm a WITCH!*

CONTENTS

Chapter 1: A SPELL FOR SMELL-A-NiE 133

Chapter 2: CRUNCHY. SALTY WAFFLES 141

Chapter 3: BRUCE 149

Chapter 4: TOADS AND MiCE 163

Chapter 5: TiM-BER! 181

Chapter 6: FRANKiE 199

Chapter 7: SHOWTiME! 217

Chapter 8: THE SPELL IS ON! 233

Chapter 9: A STAR IS BORN 243

A SPELL FOR SMELL-A-NiE

Abracadabra!

Alakazam!

Presto change-o!

Heidi Heckelbeck flipped open her *Book of Spells*. The book had been a gift from her grandmother, who was a witch. Heidi's mother was also a witch, as well as her Aunt Trudy and, of course, Heidi. Heidi's dad and little brother, Henry, were just regular people.

The book's worn pages crinkled as she thumbed through them.

"Bingo!" Heidi said to herself.

She had found the spell:

How to Make Someone Forget

Heidi had discovered it last night. Tucked inside the page was a piece

of paper. Heidi unfolded it. It was a
list of all the rotten things Melanie
Maplethorpe had done to Heidi on
her first day of school yesterday.

Mean Things Melanie
Did to Me

1. She called me smelly.

2. She gave me five dirty
looks for no reason!

3. She put a jack-o'-lantern
face on my self-portrait.

4. She made me get cast as
a scary apple tree in the
class play.

"I'm going to teach Princess Smell-a-nie a lesson once and for all," said Heidi.

In three weeks Heidi's second-grade class would be performing *The Wizard of Oz*. Heidi planned to cast the spell on opening night.

Imagine how meanie Melanie will feel when she forgets all her lines, thought Heidi. She could hardly wait.

Heidi studied the list of ingredients she would need for the spell.

1 eye of a gingerbread man

1 black plastic spider

1 piece of straw

1 teaspoon of salt

3 cornflakes

2 sour gummy worms

1 puppy tooth

1 tablespoon of catnip

3 splashes of water

Wow, thought Heidi. *Where am I going to find all this stuff?* It would be a treasure hunt, that was for sure. She copied the ingredients onto a piece of paper and stuck it in her pocket. Then she read the directions carefully.

Mix ingredients together in a red sand pail. Close your eyes and place one hand over the pail.

Hold your Witches of Westwick medallion in your other hand. Chant the following words:

Oh, SPECIAL JUICE,
LET YOUR POWERS LOOSE!
HELP ME QUICKLY,
SHOW ME SOON THE SIGNS.
MAKE [NAME OF PERSON]
FORGET [his or her] LINES!

I'd better get started, thought Heidi.

Chapter 2

CRUNCHY, SALTY WAFFLES

Heidi stashed the *Book of Spells* in her keepsake box and shoved it under the bed. Then she found a silver drawstring pouch that would hold her spell ingredients. The pouch had been a gift from Aunt Trudy. She tied it to her belt loop and dashed downstairs to the kitchen, where mom and Henry were waiting.

Mom had made waffles for breakfast. She placed a waffle and orange slices in front of Heidi.

"You know what I'm in the mood for?" asked Heidi.

"Let me guess," said Mom. "Not waffles."

"Cornflakes," said Heidi.

Heidi's mother raised an eyebrow.

"Haven't you heard?" asked Mom. "You hate cornflakes."

"I know," said Heidi, "but I'm craving crunchy waffles."

"Me too!" said Henry.

Heidi rolled her eyes.

"Do you even know what 'crave' means?" asked Heidi.

"Yup," said Henry. "It means you absolutely have to have something or else you'll go bananas."

"Wow, you're smarter than I thought," said Heidi.

Mom set a box of cornflakes on the table.

Heidi sprinkled some on her waffles.

Then she snuck a few into her pouch.

Now she needed salt. But first she had to distract Henry.

"Cool-o!" said Heidi. "There's a maze on the back of the cereal box!"

"Let me see!" said Henry.

Heidi slid the cereal box to Henry.

He studied the maze while he ate.

Heidi grabbed the saltshaker. She unscrewed the top and poured some into her pouch. Then she put the saltshaker back on the table.

Henry looked up. "Hey, Mom," he said. "Heidi just put salt on her crunchy waffles!"

"So?" said Heidi.

"So that's gross," said Henry.

Then Dad walked into the kitchen.

"I like salt on my waffles too," said Dad. "And ketchup and bacon."

Heidi and Henry groaned.

"Okay, okay," said Mom. "Hop to it, kiddos, or you'll miss the bus!"

Chapter 3

BRUCE

Heidi looked for some of the spell ingredients on the way to the bus stop. She didn't see a piece of straw or a single puppy tooth along the way. *How am I supposed to find a puppy tooth, anyway?* she wondered. Heidi had never seen one lying around before. Did puppies even lose their teeth? Heidi had no idea, but she absolutely had to have one to complete her spell.

"*Woo-hoo!*" a voice called. "Heidi! Henry!"

Aunt Trudy waved from her porch. Her cottage looked like a gingerbread house with pink and green trim. She had on a bathrobe and held a cup of tea in her hand. Her red hair was the same color as Heidi's, only Aunt Trudy wore hers in a braid. Heidi loved Aunt Trudy. She learned all kinds of cool witchy stuff from her—stuff that her mother would not share.

"Come visit me after school!" Aunt Trudy sang.

"Sure thing!" said Heidi, waving back.

Henry waved too.

The school bus pulled to the curb a few houses up. Heidi and Henry ran like crazy to catch it.

Henry hopped on board and sat next to his new friend Dudley. Henry had only taken the bus once, but he acted like an old pro. This was Heidi's first time, since her mom had given her a ride yesterday. Heidi looked around for her friend Lucy Lancaster. Lucy had been nice to Heidi on her first day of school, but there was no sign of Lucy on the bus. Then she noticed Lucy's friend Bruce Bickerson. Bruce had short brown hair and wore tortoiseshell glasses. The seat beside him was empty. Heidi tried to act cool

as she walked up the aisle. Then she sat down next to Bruce.

"Hey," said Bruce.

"Hey," said Heidi.

The bus groaned as it began to move.

"So why'd you leave your old school, anyway?" asked Bruce.

"I didn't have an old school," said Heidi. "My mom homeschooled my brother and me."

"That's so cool!" said Bruce. "Did you watch TV and play games whenever you felt like it?"

"No way," said Heidi. "We had a strict schedule, but sometimes we got to have school in our pajamas."

"Sounds comfy," said Bruce. "So, are you excited about the school play?"

"Not really," said Heidi.

"Me neither," said Bruce. "I'd rather

be working on my sticker tracker."

"What's a sticker tracker?" asked Heidi.

"It's a special sticker I invented," said Bruce. "You can stick it on letters, people—even pets. Then you can track the object on a webcam. I call it the Bicker Sticker."

"That's neat," said Heidi. "Have you tested it?"

"Yeah, I tested it on my puppy," said Bruce. "I saw him dig up my mom's tulip bulbs from my laboratory."

"You have a puppy?" asked Heidi. "And a laboratory?"

"Yup," said Bruce. "He's a white lab named Benjamin Franklin, but we call him Frankie for short. My laboratory is in the basement."

"Has Frankie lost any teeth?" asked Heidi eagerly.

"Not yet," said Bruce.

"Can I have one if he does?" asked Heidi.

"I guess so," said Bruce.

"I'll trade you a shark tooth for a puppy tooth," said Heidi.

"Deal!" said Bruce.

"Will you promise to check his puppy bed every day?" asked Heidi.

"Promise," said Bruce. "I'll track him with a Bicker Sticker too!"

They shook on it.

Heidi felt pretty good for a change, but the feeling only lasted for about a

second because soon she heard a . . .

WHACK!

A backpack smacked Bruce in the back of the head.

"Owee!" yelped Bruce.

His eyeglasses sailed across two seats and landed in the aisle.

Heidi gasped.

Who would do such a rotten thing? she wondered.

It must've been meanie Melanie. She whipped around to get a good look.

Chapter 4

TOADS AND MICE

When Heidi turned around, she came face-to-face with a squinty-eyed boy with a pug nose and freckles. He gave Heidi the evil eye. Heidi turned right back around. Her friend Bruce had his arms out like a zombie and was grasping the air. Poor Bruce! He couldn't see a thing without his glasses.

"Bickerson's *blind*!" said the bully as he laughed.

Heidi spotted Bruce's glasses on the floor. She dove down and grabbed them. As she crawled back to her seat Heidi noticed the bully's sneakers. She

gently tugged the laces and untied them. Then she jumped to her feet and handed the glasses to Bruce.

"Thanks," he said.

"No problem," said Heidi.

Kids began to file off the bus. The bully shoved his way down the aisle. But before he could get to the stairs, he tripped over his shoelaces and stumbled to the ground.

Everyone clapped and laughed.

"Did you have something to do with that?" asked Bruce.

"Maybe," said Heidi.

Bruce held up his right hand and Heidi slapped him five.

"Who was that, anyway?" asked

Heidi as they made their way off the bus.

"Travis Templeton," said Bruce. "He's a fifth grader and the biggest bully in the whole school."

Wow, thought Heidi. *School was much easier at home.*

The morning seemed to whiz by. Melanie held her nose whenever she saw Heidi, but nothing else bad happened.

Heidi had lunch with Bruce and Lucy. Next she yawned her way through drama class. When school was finally over, she was able to visit Aunt Trudy.

Heidi ran from the bus stop to Aunt Trudy's and rang the bell. Aunt Trudy's parrots squawked in the kitchen. She opened the door and gave

Heidi a squeeze. Heidi got a whiff of flowers, tea, and spice. Aunt Trudy ran a mail-order perfume business from home. She made all her perfumes and witch's brews in her kitchen.

"Come on in!" sang Aunt Trudy. "I made apple cider."

Heidi brushed through the beaded
curtains that led into the living room.

She took off her coat and sat down on the couch. Aunt Trudy's cats, Agnes and Hilda, jumped onto her lap.

Aunt Trudy sat down on a soft, mushroom-shaped stool. She gave Heidi some gingersnaps and apple cider.

"So, how's school going?" asked Aunt Trudy.

"Not so great," said Heidi.

"I know it's hard being new," said Aunt Trudy. "Tell me about it."

Heidi told Aunt Trudy about meanie Melanie and how she had gotten Heidi cast as a scary tree in the class play.

She also told her about the bully on the school bus.

"Give Melanie time," said Aunt Trudy. "She's not used to having a new girl in class. As for the bully, just ignore him. I bet if you do, he'll stop bothering you."

"I wish I could cast a spell on both of them," said Heidi. "By the way, do you have a black plastic spider?"

Aunt Trudy laughed at first. She knew exactly what Heidi was up to. But then she sighed and looked at Heidi with a raised eyebrow.

"You must be careful with your powers," said Aunt Trudy. "You can't turn people into toads and mice—or make them forget—just because they make you mad."

"I just want to scare Melanie," said Heidi. "I would reverse the spell after the play."

"Witches have to solve their problems without magic first," said Aunt Trudy. "That's why they go to school."

"Have you ever practiced magic on your customers?" asked Heidi.

"Never," said Aunt Trudy. "And you must promise me you'll never use magic at school."

Maybe her aunt was right. Maybe Heidi should just learn how to get along with others.

"Okay," agreed Heidi, but she was careful not to promise.

After their snack, Aunt Trudy had

to get back to work. She gave Heidi a hug and asked her to take out the trash before she left. Heidi carried the paper bag of trash to the barrel. On the way she noticed a cat toy on the top of the trash. She pulled it out and felt it with her fingers. It felt like it was stuffed with pine needles. Then she sniffed it.

Catnip! thought Heidi. *That's one*

of the spell ingredients. She decided to take the cat toy with her, just in case. She stuffed it in her pouch and dumped the paper bag into the barrel.

Then she ran down the sidewalk for home.

Chapter 5

TiM-BER!

Heidi stopped thinking about casting spells and worked on getting along with others. When Melanie made fun of her clothes, Heidi ignored her. When Travis gave her the evil eye, she pretended not to notice. And when Lucy wanted to be first on the monkey bars, Heidi let her go first. Heidi was

a good citizen for three whole weeks!
But then everything went bonkers at
dress rehearsal.

Heidi rubbed brown face paint on
her face and hands to look like tree

bark. Then she helped Lucy stuff her
curly dark hair into an old-lady wig.

"Hello, Auntie Em!" said Heidi.

Lucy laughed.

"You should see my Munchkin wig," said Lucy.

She pulled another wig from her backpack. It had orange curlicue hair with a rubber bald patch in front.

"Scary, right?" said Lucy.

Heidi laughed so hard she snorted.

"What's so funny?" asked Bruce.
Heidi and Lucy turned around.

Bruce had on silver face paint, silver
clothes, and a kitchen funnel on top
of his head. He held a plastic ax in his

hand. The girls laughed even harder.

"I'm the Tin Man," said Bruce. "So what?"

"So you look like you belong in a junkyard!" said Lucy.

"Well, *you* look like you belong in an old folk's home!" said Bruce.

"And Heidi looks like she belongs in a pigsty," said Melanie.

Melanie was wearing her Dorothy costume, but she acted like the Wicked Witch.

Mrs. Noddywonks, their drama teacher, clapped her hands.

"Please put on your costume, Heidi," she said.

Heidi joined two other students who were scary apple trees. They

already had on their costumes.
Mrs. Noddywonks lowered the
cardboard tree trunk over Heidi's
body. Heidi could barely move. She
had to twist the trunk to find the hole
for her face. Then she poked her arms
through the holes in either side of the
tree.

"Hold your arms in the air like branches," said Mrs. Noddywonks.

Heidi held up her arms. She felt like a total ding-dong.

"Places please, everyone!" called

Mrs. Noddywonks. "Now let's start by practicing the apple tree scene."

"Come on, Stanley!" said Melanie.

Her ruby slippers clacked down the stairs in front of the stage. She held a basket with a stuffed Toto peeking out.

Stanley Stonewrecker had the part of the Scarecrow. He was Melanie's closest friend.

"Action!" said Mrs. Noddywonks.

Dorothy ran up the stairs onto the stage.

"Oh, look!" she said. "Apples!"

She tried to pick an apple from one

of the trees, but it slapped her hand.

"Ouch!" cried Dorothy.

"Get your grubby paws off my apples!" said the tree.

"Did you say something?" asked Dorothy. "We don't have talking trees in Kansas!"

"Go pick on someone else!" said the tree.

"Yeah!" said the second tree.

Heidi watched from the hole in her tree.

"Come on, Dorothy," said the Scarecrow. "You don't want to eat *those* wormy apples."

"How dare you make fun of my apples!" said the first tree. "Fire away, guys!"

The trees launched their Styrofoam apples.

Dorothy and the Scarecrow dodged the apples. They also picked up a few for Dorothy's basket. When Dorothy stood up, she bumped one of Heidi's

branches on purpose. Heidi's costume
shifted to one side.

"Help!" cried Heidi. "I can't see!"

She teetered one way and then
tottered the other. She turned in

circles, and then *splat!* Heidi tipped
over on center stage.

"*Tim-ber!*" said Melanie. She nudged
Stanley and they both laughed.

Heidi could hear Mrs. Noddywonks

scurry across the stage. She pulled
Heidi's costume off.

"Are you okay, dear?" asked
Mrs. Noddywonks.

Heidi's hair was tangled and
stuck to her face paint. She felt too
embarrassed to notice if she was hurt.

"I'm fine," said Heidi.

But Heidi wasn't fine, she was FURIOUS.

That Melanie needed to learn a lesson once and for all.

Chapter 6

FRANKiE

The spell was BACK ON! Tomorrow was opening night, and Heidi had to find the rest of the ingredients. She still needed:

◖		
	1 eye of a gingerbread man	
	1 black plastic spider	
	1 piece of straw	

1 teaspoon of salt

3 cornflakes

2 sour gummy worms

1 puppy tooth

1 tablespoon of catnip

3 splashes of water

Heidi studied the list. *Candy will be easy,* she thought. She ran to the kitchen pantry and found the plastic Halloween pumpkins. She dumped the leftover candy on the floor and sifted through mini candy bars and loose candy corn. Then, like a glittering gem in a treasure chest, Heidi uncovered a black plastic spider.

"Yes!" said Heidi as she held up her
find.

"Not so fast!" said Henry, who was
standing in the doorway. "That's
MINE."

"Finders keepers," said Heidi.

"Give it," said Henry. "Or I'll tell."

"Wait," said Heidi. "I'll trade my mini lightsaber I got at the Burger Pit."

"Done!" said Henry.

"It's on my nightstand," said Heidi.

Henry bolted upstairs.

Phew, thought Heidi. But she still needed sour gummy worms. Heidi's mother loved sour gummies— gummy worms, gummy bears, you name it. Heidi tiptoed across the kitchen and pulled open her mother's secret candy drawer. She saw butter-scotch candies and mints. *They have*

to be in here somewhere, she thought. She reached farther into the drawer. Her hand hit something. *Aha!* Heidi pulled out a small crumpled bag from the back of the drawer. She peeked inside. She saw red licorice and sour gummy worms.

"Score!" said Heidi.

She quickly stuffed two sour gummy worms into her pouch and one into her mouth.

"Heidi!" called Mom. "Time to go!"

Heidi shoved the bag back in the drawer.

"Okay!" said Heidi, trying to act normal.

Heidi had a playdate with Bruce.

He had asked her over to see his laboratory.

Mom drove Heidi to Bruce's house. He answered the door in his white lab coat and safety glasses. His puppy, Frankie, wagged his tail and barked at Heidi.

Heidi let Frankie sniff her hand.

"Has he lost any teeth yet?" asked Heidi.

"Not that I know of," said Bruce.

Heidi followed Bruce down to the basement. She looked around at all his experiments. Bruce had built a robot, and a tornado made out of

chicken wire and cotton balls. Some things were labeled TOP SECRET.

"Would you like to see how the Bicker Sticker works?" asked Bruce.

"Sure!" said Heidi.

Bruce tapped some keys on his computer. Heidi watched the screen. She saw something moving.

"That's Frankie," said Bruce.

Heidi couldn't see Frankie, but she could see what he was doing.

"Is he supposed to be eating hamburger buns?" asked Heidi.

Bruce looked closely at the screen.

"Oh no!" he said. "Come on!"

Heidi and Bruce raced up the stairs to the kitchen. There they found Frankie happily munching on hamburger rolls and wagging his tail.

Bruce tugged on the bag of rolls. Frankie growled playfully.

"Give him a chew toy!" said Bruce.

Heidi spotted a basket of chew toys and grabbed a plastic pork chop.

"Here, Frankie!" said Heidi, waving the pork chop back and forth.

Frankie had no interest in the fake pork chop. He barked and whined at the hamburger rolls, which were now on the counter.

Heidi was about to toss the pork chop back into the basket when she noticed something stuck in the side. It was a tooth!

"I found a puppy tooth in the chew toy!" said Heidi.

"Let me see!" said Bruce.

Heidi picked the tooth out of the

pork chop and handed it to Bruce.

"That's so cool," said Bruce.

He pulled a magnifying glass out of his lab coat to get a better look.

"May I still trade you for a shark tooth?" asked Heidi. She tried not to sound too eager.

"Sure," said Bruce. "I'd much rather have a shark tooth any day."

He handed the tooth to Heidi, and she popped it into her pouch. Now she had nearly all the ingredients for her spell. Just three more to go, and a sand pail.

"I promise to bring a shark tooth to school tomorrow," said Heidi.

"Cool," said Bruce.

Then they thumped back down the stairs to the basement to check out some more science experiments.

SHOWTIME!

Butterflies!

Jitterbugs!

Showtime!

Well, almost. Heidi had four hours before opening night. She still had to find a couple more spell ingredients. The splashes of water would be easy. So would the sand pail. The piece of straw and the eye of a gingerbread man would be trickier.

After school Heidi's mother took Henry and Heidi to Lulu's Bakery. Mom

had ordered cupcakes for the cast party. Heidi prayed she would find the eye of a gingerbread man at the bakery. This would be her only chance.

Heidi stayed up front while Henry and Mom followed Lulu to the back of the store. When they were far enough away, Heidi turned to the lady behind the counter.

"Do you have any eyes for gingerbread people?" she whispered.

The lady thought for a moment. "They're out of season," she said, "but I'll check."

She opened and closed several little drawers. Then she pulled out a small strip of paper. The paper was dotted with tiny sets of candy eyes.

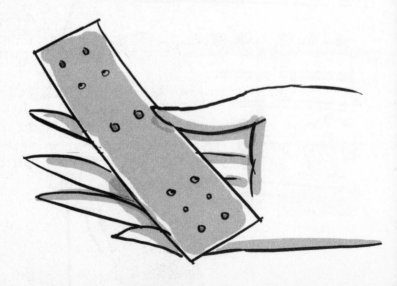

"How many do you need?" asked the lady.

"Just one," said Heidi.

"One eye?" asked the lady.

One eye *did* sound kind of strange.

"I mean, one pair," said Heidi.

"Here," said the lady. "Take what's left on the sheet."

"How much?" asked Heidi.

"No charge," said the lady, and she handed the strip of candy eyes to Heidi.

"Thank you!" said Heidi.

She gently folded the paper and put it in her pouch.

Lulu carried the cupcakes to the counter. Each cupcake had a *Wizard of Oz* topper.

"I want Toto!" said Henry.

"I want the ruby slippers!" said Heidi.

Heidi's mom paid for the cupcakes, and then they went home to pick up Dad.

"I forgot something in the house," said Heidi.

"Make it fast," said Mom. "You don't want to be late on opening night!"

Inside, Heidi carefully placed her pouch, her medallion, measuring spoons, a bottle of water, a spoon, and a pair of scissors in a shopping bag. Then she raced to the garage and unstacked the sand pails. She tossed a red one in the shopping bag. Then she zoomed to the cleaning closet and

plucked a bristle from the broom.

Oh no, thought Heidi. *These dumb bristles are made of plastic, not straw. How can a house with two witches have a fake broom?*

Heidi slammed the closet door behind her. She had everything she needed except for one crummy piece of straw. Now her spell was ruined. She grabbed her shopping bag anyway and ran to the car.

At school Heidi ignored everyone backstage. She put on her makeup and tree costume. Then she peeked around the curtain to see if Aunt Trudy had arrived. As she looked out at the audience someone pushed her from behind. Heidi stumbled onstage as Melanie and Stanley cracked up

behind the curtain. Heidi whirled around. She tried to find the split in the curtain, but all she found was more fabric. Then Lucy opened the curtain and yanked Heidi backstage.

"Are you okay?" asked Lucy.

Heidi wanted to scream. But then she looked at Stanley and got an idea.

"Help me out of my costume," said Heidi. "I have to use the bathroom."

Lucy lifted the tree trunk over Heidi's head.

"Hurry up!" said Lucy. "The play is about to start."

"I'll only be a sec," said Heidi.

Heidi grabbed her shopping bag. As she walked past Stanley she plucked a piece of straw from his scarecrow costume.

This will do the trick, she thought.

Then Heidi smiled wickedly.

Now she had everything she needed to cast her spell.

Chapter 8

THE SPELL IS ON!

Heidi hid in a bathroom stall and set the sand pail on the toilet seat. She peeled a candy eye from the strip of paper and dropped it in the pail. Then she added the spider, the straw, the gummy worms, the puppy tooth, and the three cornflakes.

Heidi measured
a teaspoon of salt
and added it to
the mix.

And then she
snipped a tiny
hole in the cat
toy and added
one tablespoon
of catnip.

She added three splashes of water and mixed the ingredients together with a spoon.

Then Heidi closed her eyes. She put her right hand over the pail and held the medallion in her left hand. Heidi chanted the words of the spell:

Oh special juice,
let your powers loose!
Help me quickly;
show me soon the signs.
Make Melanie Maplethorpe
forget her lines!

Now the joke will be on Melanie, thought Heidi.

Heidi gathered her things and headed backstage. The play had just started, and there was Melanie onstage, scratching her head. She couldn't remember her lines. The spell had worked!

Mrs. Noddywonks gave Melanie her opening line. "Oh, Toto," she said. "I wish I could go somewhere over the rainbow."

Melanie tried to repeat the words, but she forgot them again.

Kids backstage whispered and

laughed. Melanie's face turned red. She began to cry.

Mrs. Noddywonks ran onstage.

"Ladies and gentlemen," she said, "we're going to take a short break and be right back."

The curtain squeaked as it closed.

Mrs. Noddywonks put her arm around Melanie. "It's only the jitters," she said. "Take a deep breath."

"What's the matter with me?" Melanie wailed. "How did I become a terrible Dorothy?"

Just then something strange happened. Something so crazy, Heidi

had to pinch herself. She—Heidi
Heckelbeck—felt sorry for Melanie.

How can this be? she wondered.
Melanie is my worst enemy! But
Heidi couldn't bear to see Melanie so
upset. Heidi knew what that felt like,
and now she had made someone else
feel the same way. There was only
one thing to do.

Chapter 9

A STAR IS BORN

Heidi ran back to the bathroom with her things. She entered a stall and set the red pail on the toilet seat. Heidi put her right hand over the pail and held her medallion in her left hand. Then she closed her eyes and reversed the spell.

Thank you.
Thank you.
Now all is well.
Undo my work
and reverse the spell.

As soon as Heidi walked out of the bathroom, she heard Melanie's voice.

"I remember my lines!" Melanie shouted.

"Oh good. . . . Thank heavens!" said

Mrs. Noddywonks. "Okay, children, take your places!"

After that, nobody tripped and no one forgot a single line.

At the end everyone came out
onstage for their bows. Heidi could
hear her dad cheering for her from

the audience. *The play wasn't so bad,* thought Heidi. But she was glad it was over!

"You were the best scary tree ever!" said Dad as he handed Heidi a cupcake with the ruby slippers on top.

"I want one too!" said Henry.

"Me too," said Mom.

"We'll be right back," said Dad as he, Mom, and Henry set off on a cupcake hunt.

Then Aunt Trudy gave Heidi a big hug.

"Isn't it a bit strange that Melanie forgot her lines?" asked Aunt Trudy. "And then suddenly—just like that— she remembered them! I can't explain it. Can you?"

Heidi looked at the floor. Aunt Trudy knew exactly what Heidi had done.

"Did you learn something?" asked Aunt Trudy.

"Yes," said Heidi. "It feels terrible to make someone unhappy."

"Good girl," said Aunt Trudy.

"But how come Melanie's mean to me?" asked Heidi.

"That's Melanie's problem," said Aunt Trudy. "Not yours. And hopefully someday Melanie will learn how to be kind too."

And that, along with her cupcake

with the ruby slippers on top, made
Heidi feel like a star.

CONTENTS

Chapter 1: ME WANT COO-KiE! 257

Chapter 2: BA-BA-BORiNG! 271

Chapter 3: RAZZLE-DAZZLE! 283

Chapter 4: DAD FAiNTS 291

Chapter 5: THE MAGiC TOUCH 303

Chapter 6: THE COOKiE CHARM 315

Chapter 7: P.U. 329

Chapter 8: STiNK! STANK! STUNK! 339

Chapter 9: COUGH DROPS 355

Chapter 10: WOOF! 365

ME WANT COO-KiE!

Yum!

Yummy!

Yummers!

Heidi Heckelbeck had cookies on her mind. She had just signed up for the Brewster Elementary cookie contest. Heidi had never entered a contest before. She wondered if she would win. She had won a raffle one time, but that had been super-easy. All she'd had to do was write her name on a strip of paper and stick it in a box with some other names.

The prize had been a silver turtle necklace. Winning had been fun, and now, more than anything, Heidi wanted to win the school cookie contest.

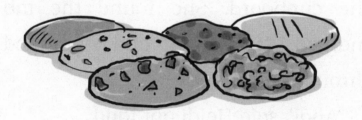

What kind of cookies should I make? wondered Heidi. She could make oatmeal raisin, but raisins were kind of squishy and gross. Peanut butter cookies were good, but not her favorite. *How about chocolate chunk?*

Chocolate chunk would be a winner, thought Heidi. They were also her favorite.

Heidi hopped onto a step stool and grabbed the family recipe box from the cupboard. She found the tab marked "Desserts" and thumbed through the recipes.

"Aha!" said Heidi out loud.

"Aha, what?" asked Heidi's mom as she walked into the kitchen.

"I found our famous chocolate chunk cookie recipe," said Heidi. "I entered a cookie contest at school. It's this Saturday."

"Need some help?" asked Mom.

"Do I EVER," said Heidi. "I've never made cookies all by myself."

"Let's gather the ingredients first," said Mom.

Henry, Heidi's five-year-old brother, ran into the kitchen. "Can I help?"

"No," said Heidi firmly. "These cookies have to be made by ME."

"Then can I be your taste-tester?" asked Henry.

"Ha! Are you kidding?" asked Heidi. "That would be like hiring the Cookie Monster."

Then Henry pretended to be the Cookie Monster.

"Me want COO-kie! Munch! Munch! Chomp! Chomp!"

Heidi rolled her eyes. Then she looked at the recipe. "Three cups of flour," she said.

Heidi lugged a tub of flour from

the pantry and plopped it on the counter. Mom got the white sugar, brown sugar, and chocolate chunks. Heidi got two sticks of butter from the fridge. They laid out all the ingredients on the counter. Then Mom got the mixer, the measuring spoons, and the measuring cups.

"Oh no," said Heidi. "We're out of eggs."

"That's okay," said Mom. "I'll pick some eggs up on the way home from school tomorrow. If we make the cookies in the evening, they'll be nice and fresh for the contest the next day."

"Good idea," said Heidi.

"So, what do you get if you win?" asked Henry.

"You get to have your picture and your recipe published in the town newspaper," said Heidi.

"That's it?" said Henry. "No cash prizes or giveaways?"

"Well, there IS one giveaway," said

Heidi. "The winner can *give away* her brother for a year of free cookies."

"Ha-ha. Very funny," said Henry. "But if you gave me away, you would probably miss me."

"Maybe a teeny bit," said Heidi.

Henry smiled. "Does that mean the taste-tester gets to have his picture in the paper too?"

"Don't push it, little dude," said Heidi.

Chapter 2

BA-BA-BORING!

At school everybody was talking about the cookie contest. Stanley Stonewrecker was going to make Heavenly Surprise cookies. Charlie Chen was going to make toasted s'mores cookies. Natalie Newman was going to make pumpkin whoopie pies with cream cheese filling. *Wow,* thought Heidi as she put her things in her cubby. *Everyone else's cookies sound so fancy.* Heidi began to wonder if her cookies were special enough.

Heidi walked over to her friend Lucy Lancaster. "What kind are *you* making?" Heidi asked Lucy.

"Sugar cookies," said Lucy. "With Fruity Polka Dots cereal on top."

"Yum," said Heidi.

"What kind are *you* making?" asked Lucy.

"Chocolate chunk," said Heidi.

"Ew," said Melanie Maplethorpe.

Melanie was Heidi's worst enemy. She had been listening in.

Heidi turned around. "What's your problem?" she asked.

"YOUR COOKIES!" said Melanie. "I mean, how blah can you get? Even Girl Scout cookies are more exciting than THAT."

Lucy put her hands on her hips and glared at Melanie. "What kind are *you* going to make?" asked Lucy. "Disgusting chip? Or oatmeal poison?"

"Neither," said Melanie. "I'm going to make cinnamon swirl cookies with toffee bits. My ingredients had to be *special ordered*. And by the way, I'm SO going to win."

Then Melanie did a little twirl and walked off with her nose in the air.

"Well, whoop-de-do," said Lucy to Melanie's bouncing ponytail.

Heidi sighed. "It's true," she said. "My chocolate chunk cookies DO sound boring next to yours and Melanie's."

"Chocolate chunk cookies are NOT boring," said Lucy. "Stick with what you do best and you'll come out on top."

On top of what? thought Heidi. *The garbage heap? Hmm . . . Maybe I need to come up with a fancier kind of cookie.*

A few minutes later Heidi's teacher, Mrs. Welli, handed out contest rules and entry forms. Heidi decided to give her boring cookies a new name. On her entry form, she wrote, "Magical Chocolate Chunk Cookies." *That sounds a teeny bit better than plain chocolate chunk,* she thought. Then she handed it in.

Later in gym, Heidi's class did the Wacky Obstacle Course. Bruce Bickerson and Heidi were partners. Together, they jumped through a pretend flaming hoop. They walked the balance beam over a pit of crocodiles. They zip-lined across a steep valley. In the middle of the *Indiana Jones*

snake-filled tunnel, Heidi asked Bruce what kind of cookies he was going to make for the contest on Saturday.

"Mega Mint," said Bruce. "They're chocolate cookies with vanilla chips and crushed peppermints."

"Wow," said Heidi. "They sound amazing."

"They're insane," said Bruce. "But some people think they taste like toothpaste."

Heidi didn't think Bruce's cookies sounded anything like toothpaste. They sounded mega-tasty. Everybody's cookies sounded great except hers. There was no way crummy ol' chocolate chunk cookies would win the contest. She had to come up with something new—something different. *But what?* thought Heidi as she crawled out of the tunnel and lined up with her classmates.

Heidi was sure of one thing: She just *had* to outshine Melanie Maplethorpe. That mean girl didn't deserve to win anything.

Chapter 3

RAZZLE-DAZZLE!

When Heidi got home, she raided the pantry. She grabbed pretzels, mini marshmallows, jelly beans, a box of old candy canes, and Peanut Butter Crunch cereal. She piled everything onto the counter with her other cookie ingredients.

"What are you doing?" asked Henry.

"Jazzing up my cookie recipe."

"What for?"

"So I can beat Melanie," replied Heidi. "She's making cinnamon swirl cookies with toffee bits."

"Do they taste good?" asked Henry.

"She had to SPECIAL ORDER her ingredients," said Heidi.

"But do they *taste good*?"

"How should *I* know?" said Heidi.

"Maybe they're gross."

"I doubt it," said Heidi. "Everything Smell-a-nie does is perfect."

"But OUR chocolate chunk cookie recipe is perfect too," said Henry.

Heidi folded her arms and looked at Henry. "Melanie laughed when she heard I was going to make chocolate chunk cookies."

"Has she tasted our cookies?"

"No."

"She should," said Henry. "They're

the best-tasting cookies in the whole world."

"Who made YOU a cookie judge?"

"I did," said Henry.

"But you like animal crackers," said Heidi. "A real cookie judge would know that animal crackers are not good cookies."

"They're called animal CRACKERS. They're not even cookies. Besides, I can tell the difference between a good cookie and a bad cookie."

"Well, I want to make a blue-ribbon cookie," said Heidi.

"Then you should make our Heckel-beck Chocolate Chunk Cookies," said Henry. "They're the BEST!"

"You said it!" said Mom.

"Let's get started!" said Dad.

Heidi's mom and dad had walked into the kitchen during Heidi and Henry's discussion. Her parents both had on aprons. Dad handed an apron to Heidi. Heidi had never worn an apron before. She took the apron and slipped it over her head. Mom tied the sash in the back. All of a sudden Heidi began to feel like a real cook.

Now all she had to do was make a first-place, blue-ribbon cookie.

Chapter 4

DAD FAINTS

Heidi's dad switched on the oven. Then he pointed at the pretzels, candy, and cereal sitting on the counter.

"What's all this?" asked Dad.

"Magical ingredients," said Heidi.

"Heidi wants to jazz up the family cookie recipe," said Henry.

Dad was puzzled. "What for?"

"Because it's SO blah," said Heidi.

Dad pretended to faint into Mom's arms. Mom struggled to hold him up.

"Heidi, look what you've done to your father," said Mom.

"What did she do?" asked Henry.

Heidi looked at her dad.

He opened one eye and peeked at Heidi. Then he coughed and sputtered.

"I just want to add a little zing," said Heidi. "What's the big deal?"

Dad stood and rolled up his sleeves. "Is that the *real* reason you want to add junk food to our cookies?" he asked.

Heidi looked at the floor.

"Do you think our recipe is missing something?" asked Dad.

"Bingo," said Heidi.

Dad was surprised. "Heidi, this

is not just *any* recipe. I've worked on it for *years*. These cookies are something special."

Heidi still looked doubtful. "What makes them so special?"

"Let me show you," said Dad. He switched on the stove. "First we need to brown the butter."

"What's so special about that?" asked Heidi.

"Wait and see," said Dad.

Heidi unwrapped the butter and dropped them into a pan. Soon the butter began to sizzle. Heidi stirred it around. After a while the butter began to bubble. Dad took it off the flame.

"Smell," said Dad.

Heidi and Henry both sniffed the browned butter.

"Smells good," said Heidi.

"Like toffee," said Henry.

"Exactly," said Dad. "Browning the butter gives the cookies a toasty toffee flavor. That makes them stand apart from other chocolate chunk cookies."

Heidi beat the browned butter, the sugars, the flour, and the vanilla. She cracked two eggs into the batter and mixed them in. Dad added an extra yolk to the bowl.

"An extra yolk will make them soft and chewy," said Dad.

Heidi swirled in the yolk.

"I also add two kinds of chocolate," said Dad. "Milk chocolate and semi-sweet. That's another special twist."

Heidi yawned. Dad's special steps

didn't sound very exciting. If he had asked her to add some chopped-up candy bars and rainbow sprinkles, *that* would've sounded exciting.

Dad handed Heidi an ice-cream scoop. She scooped the cookie dough and squeezed the handle. Mounds of dough plopped onto the greased cookie sheet.

"Now we'll bake them at a very high heat," said Dad. "And we'll only cook them for four minutes. This will make them golden on the outside and like cookie dough on the inside."

Heidi set the timer for four minutes. Then she and Henry stood on two chairs and watched the cookies bake.

Dad got out fancy dessert plates. Mom laid out napkins. When the cookies were done, Heidi slid one onto each plate.

Then it was time to taste them.

They all took a bite at the same time.

"Mmmmmmmm," everyone said. Everyone—except Heidi, that is.

Chapter 5

THE MAGiC TOUCH

Honk . . . shoooo!

Honk . . . shoooo!

Snoresville, USA.

Heidi carried the rest of her sample cookie to her bedroom on a napkin. She still thought the recipe was B.O.R.I.N.G., but she wanted to think about it alone. She flopped onto her beanbag chair. *Am I being unfair?* she wondered. After all, Dad *did* work on soda recipes for a living. He must know *something*. Heidi studied her cookie. It gave her an idea. What if

she pretended to be a professional cookie judge? Then she could judge the cookie fairly. Maybe she would see it in a new way.

Heidi fished around in her back-pack and pulled out the contest rules.

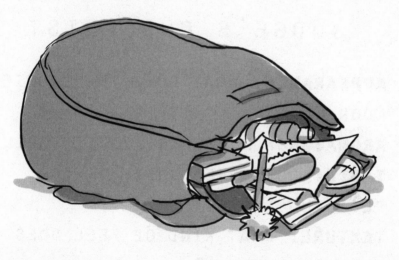

At the bottom of the page she found the Judge's Checklist. Heidi grabbed a

scented pencil from her pencil case.
It had a sugar cookie smell. Then she
looked at the scorecard.

  Scorecard ✓

JUDGE'S CHECKLIST

APPEARANCE: WHAT DOES THE COOKIE
LOOK LIKE?
AROMA: HOW DOES THE COOKIE SMELL?
TASTE: DOES THE COOKIE HAVE A
PLEASING TASTE?
TEXTURE: WHAT KIND OF FEEL DOES
THE COOKIE HAVE?
CREATIVITY: WHAT MAKES THIS
COOKIE STAND OUT?

A judge has to be super-honest, thought Heidi. Then she took a good, hard look at her cookie. *Hmmm, how does this cookie look?* she asked herself. She tried to pretend she was judging somebody else's cookie.

APPEARANCE:

CHECK ONE:

☐ EXCELLENT ☐ GOOD ☑ FAIR ☐ POOR

Heidi looked at the cookie. She wrote:

This cookie is the color tan. Tan is a boring color. If I saw this cookie at a bakery, I would say, "NEXT!"

Heidi sniffed the cookie and wrote:

This cookie does not smell like dead fish—that's the good news! The bad news is that it smells like a plain ol' everyday chocolate chunk cookie.

Heidi took a bite of her cookie. She thought hard about how it tasted. Then she wrote:

Thankfully, this cookie does not taste like liver. It tastes ho-hum. Who hasn't tasted a chocolate chunk cookie before?

Heidi took another bite of her cookie and thought about the feeling of the cookie. Then she wrote:

This cookie is not rubbery or slimy or anything gross. It's crisp on the outside and chewy on the inside with little bursts of chocolate.

See, Heidi said to herself, *I'm being fair and honest. I found something good to say about this cookie.*

The last question was the hardest.

CREATIVITY:
CHECK ONE:
☐ EXCELLENT ☐ GOOD ☐ FAIR ☑ POOR

Heidi stared at what was left of her cookie. Then she wrote:

This cookie lacks pizzazz. Where are all the wow-ee colors? Where are the zany ingredients? It's not even a fun shape. What this cookie needs is a touch of magic.

Suddenly Heidi's eyes lit up.

"THAT'S IT!" she shouted. "All my cookie needs is a magic touch!"

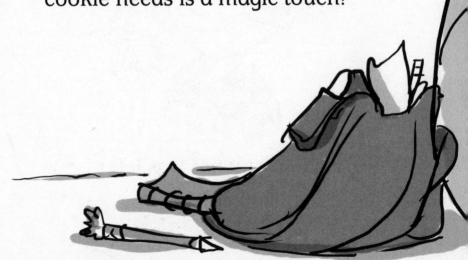

Chapter 6

THE COOKiE CHARM

Zip!

Zap!

Zing!

Heidi pulled her *Book of Spells* out from under her bed. She flipped through the pages and found a chapter called "Zesty Recipe Makeovers."

"NOW we're talking," said Heidi.

Then she noticed the perfect spell.

The Cookie Charm

Are your cookies ho-hum? Do they have the look and feel of a hockey puck? Are you the kind of witch who burns your cookies to a crisp? Then this is the spell for you! No ovens! No pans! No mess! No fuss!

It was called The Cookie Charm.

She read it over.

Ingredients:
Your baked cookies
Your favorite additional
cookie ingredients
1 cup vegetable oil
2 teaspoons pure vanilla
A dash of nutmeg

Put your baked cookies in an empty container. Add the vegetable oil, vanilla, nutmeg, and favorite cookie ingredients. Hold your Witches of Westwick medallion in your left hand.

Place your right hand over the mix. Chant the following words:

Heidi shoved her *Book of Spells* under her pillow. Then she cracked open the door. She could hear Mom helping Henry in the tub.

She crept downstairs and peeked around the corner. Dad was reading by the fire. She snuck into the kitchen

and pulled a shopping bag from the cupboard. Heidi placed the tin of chocolate chunk cookies in the bag. Then she tiptoed into the pantry and grabbed the jelly beans and mini marshmallows. Next she gathered the other spell ingredients, along with a teaspoon and a measuring cup. She dumped everything in the shopping bag.

Now what else can I add? Heidi wondered. *I know!* She opened the fridge and grabbed a chunk of cheese.

Now, THIS is what I call zing, she thought as she dropped it into her bag.

"Ahem!"

Heidi froze.

Oh no! she thought. *I'm SO busted!*

But no one was there. It had only been Dad clearing his throat in the other room. *Phew,* thought Heidi. Then she zoomed to her room and locked the door.

Heidi laid her spell ingredients

on the floor. She opened the tin of chocolate chunk cookies. Then she poured the spell ingredients on top. *They look more colorful already!* thought Heidi. *My cookies are going to blow Smell-a-nie's cookies away!*

Heidi put on her medallion. She held it in her left hand and put her right hand over the mix. Then she chanted the spell. The cookies began to bubble. Heidi covered them and looked at the clock. It was nine p.m. The cookies would be done in twelve

hours—that would make it nine in the morning. *Perfect,* thought Heidi. *The contest is at eleven.* Heidi snuck into the kitchen and put back the tin of cookies, teaspoon, and measuring cup. She was ready for the contest. Now she had to get ready for bed.

Chapter 7

P.U.

Heidi's eyes popped open. It was nine o'clock on the dot! That meant her spell was all done! She hopped out of bed and ran to the kitchen in her kitty cat pajamas. She pulled the lid off of the cookie tin and peeked at her cookies.

Wow! she thought. *It WORKED!*

Heidi's cookies had a beautiful shape—round and plump. The jelly beans, marshmallows, and chocolate looked like they had been perfectly placed. The swirls of cheese added a nice touch. There was only one thing that was a little odd: the smell.

"P.U.," said Heidi, waving her hand in front of her nose.

She closed the lid. *Well, no big deal,* she thought. *My nose isn't used*

to smelling cookies first thing in the morning. Plus I'm still sleepy. I'm sure my cookies are okay. They definitely LOOK amazing! They might even win!

"Hey, missy," said Mom, who had just walked into the kitchen with Henry. "Are you sneaking cookies before breakfast?"

Heidi jumped. "No way. I was just making sure Henry hadn't snuck any."

"Are you calling me a thief?" asked Henry.

"Well, it wouldn't be the first time," said Heidi.

"Cool it, you two," said Mom. "Or there won't be any surprise."

"Surprise?" questioned Heidi.

"What surprise?" asked Henry.

"Dad got doughnuts for breakfast," said Mom.

Heidi and Henry looked around the kitchen and spotted a pink box on the counter.

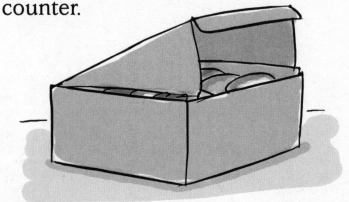

"I get the rainbow sprinkles one!" said Heidi, running for the box.

"I get the twisty kind!" said Henry, right behind her.

"I'll get the plates!" said Mom.

Mom put plates on the table. She also brought over an empty silver tray and a doily.

"What's that for?" asked Heidi.

"It's for your cookie display," said Mom.

"Fancy," said Heidi as she sank her teeth into a soft, sweet doughnut.

"We can set up the cookies on the tray when we get there," said Mom.

"When can we leave?" asked Heidi.

"As soon as everyone's ready," said Mom.

After breakfast Heidi put on her green skirt and her T-shirt with silver stars. Then she pulled on her black-and-white-striped tights and

black sneakers. Heidi looked in the mirror. She wondered what it would feel like to win first place. She practiced a winning smile in the mirror.

"Time to go!" called Dad.

Heidi thundered down the stairs, grabbed her tin of blue-ribbon cook-ies, and jumped into the car.

Chapter 8

STINK! STANK! STUNK!

A large white party tent had been set up in the middle of Brewster Elementary's playing field. There were also two smaller tents—one for sign-in and another to sell drinks. All the tents had balloons hanging inside and out. A banner across the front of the big tent read BREWSTER ELEMENTARY COOKIE CONTEST.

Heidi could see the judges' table underneath the big tent. It had a red-and-white-checked tablecloth with ruffles around the bottom. There were three chairs behind the table—one for each judge. On either side of the

judges' table were the display tables. *Wow*, thought Heidi. *This is a BIG deal.*

Heidi ran to the sign-in tent. She got entry number twelve. Heidi slipped the ticket with her number into her pocket. Then she skipped to the display table with her family close behind. Mom set the silver tray on

the table and placed the doily on top. Heidi opened her cookie tin. A funky smell floated from the container.

Henry pinched his nose. "Ew. What's that smell?"

"It's the smell of blue-ribbon cookies," said Heidi proudly.

"It smells more like dog poop," said Henry.

"That's so funny I forgot to laugh,"

said Heidi as she began to place the cookies on the tray.

Heidi's mom and dad also took a step back from the cookies. Dad fanned his nose with his hand.

"What happened to the cookies?" asked Dad.

"I snazzed them up," said Heidi.

Mom raised an eyebrow. *"Heiii-di,"* she said slowly. "Just *how* did you snazz them up?"

"Oh, you know," said Heidi, avoiding the question.

Unfortunately, Mom *did* know.

"Heidi, you know the rule," Mom said firmly. "No witching skills in your everyday life."

Heidi sighed loudly. "But how else was I going to make my cookies better?"

Dad rolled his eyes. "You still don't get it, do you?" he said.

"Get what?" asked Heidi.

"Never mind," said Dad.

"All right, we'll talk about this later,"

said Mom. Then she changed the subject. "So, what kind of cheese did you use?"

"The one with the blue spots," said Heidi.

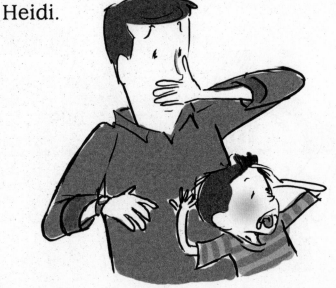

"The stinky cheese?" asked Dad.

"You mean the dog poop cheese!" said Henry.

"Stop it!" said Heidi. "I think my cookies look great."

"They *do* look great," said Mom. Then in a much lower voice she said, "But they stink to high heaven."

Heidi filled out a card with the name of her cookies and her entry number. She put it in front of her tray.

MAGICAL CHOCOLATE
CHUNK COOKIES
A Chocolate-y Chees-y
Marshmallow and Jelly Bean Delight

ENTRY NUMBER 12

"You forgot your name," said Henry.

"Did not," said Heidi. "The judges only allow entry numbers."

"Lucky for you!" said Henry.

"Why?" asked Heidi.

"Then no one will know that YOU brought the stinky cookies," said Henry.

I don't give one hoot what my family thinks about my cookies, thought Heidi as she looked for Lucy. Heidi spotted her setting up her cookies at another table. Melanie Maplethorpe was working right next to her.

"Hey, Lucy!" said Heidi.

"Hey," said Lucy.

"Where are the Fruity Polka Dots?" asked Heidi, looking over Lucy's cookies.

"I decided not to use them," said Lucy. "They tasted better plain."

"You made *plain* sugar cookies?" said Heidi.

"Yup," said Lucy. "Why? What's wrong?"

"I'll tell you what's wrong," said Melanie Maplethorpe, butting in. "They sound positively BOR-ing!"

Lucy looked crushed.

Heidi felt sorry for Lucy, but this time she kind of agreed with Melanie.

Plain sugar cookies did sound dull. The Fruity Polka Dots cereal would have put her cookies over the top. Now Lucy had no chance of winning. But Heidi didn't dare say anything.

She didn't want to hurt Lucy's feelings.

"Come on, Lucy," said Heidi. "Let's check out some of the other cookies."

Heidi and Lucy linked arms, and off they went.

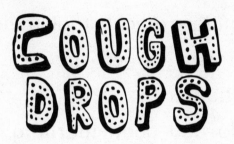

COUGH DROPS

Heidi and Lucy waved at Bruce. He was standing beside Brewster's school bell. The bell ringer started the contest, and this year Bruce had been chosen to ring the bell. Principal Pennypacker's assistant, Mrs. Crosby, gave him the signal. Bruce pulled the string.

Bong!

Bong!

Bong!

The judges quickly took their seats. Mrs. Crosby tapped the top of the microphone.

"Hello and good morning, every-

one," she began. "Welcome to the annual Brewster Elementary Cookie Contest. Here are this year's superstar judges: Jennifer Childs, our town newspaper's food editor! Brewster Elementary's Principal Pennypacker! And Lou Billings, Brewster's mayor! Now, let the judging begin!"

Everyone clapped and whistled.

Heidi grabbed Lucy's hand and squeezed it. They watched as the judges sampled cookies and made notes on the scorecards. The judges kept straight faces when they tasted the cookies—even when they tasted Melanie's yummy-sounding cinnamon swirl cookies with toffee bits.

But when they got to Heidi's cook-ies, the judges began to make funny faces.

Suddenly the principal's eyes bugged out and he grabbed his throat.

The food editor from the *Brewster Daily* looked like she had eaten rat poison.

And the mayor of Brewster began
to have a coughing fit.

It got so bad that Mrs. Crosby had to
run and get a jug of water. The mayor
gulped the water straight from the jug.

"Heidi, did you put pepper in your
cookies?" asked Lucy.

"No," said Heidi.

"Then what's going on?"

"I dunno," said Heidi. "They kind of have a funny smell. . . ."

"Like what?" asked Lucy.

"Like stinky gym socks," said Heidi.

"How come your cookies smell like gym socks?" asked Lucy.

"Maybe it's the cheese," said Heidi. "I added cheese to the recipe."

"Oh, Heidi," said Lucy. "Why didn't you just stick with plain chocolate chunk?"

Heidi looked at the mayor. He was still gulping down water.

"I wanted my cookies to stand out," she said.

"Oh, they stand out all right," said Lucy.

The mayor finally stopped coughing. His face had turned bright red,
but he looked okay. Mrs. Crosby gave
him a cough drop. *Phew*, thought
Heidi. Then she told herself that it
was no big deal. Anyone could choke
on a cookie.

Right?

WOOF!

The judges took FOREVER.

"I'm going bonkers," said Heidi.

"Me too," said Lucy.

"Do you think Melanie will win?"

"Probably," said Lucy.

"Hey, look!" said Heidi, pointing at one of the display tables.

"Oh my gosh!" said Lucy.

Bruce's dog, Frankie, had grabbed a tablecloth in his teeth. He tugged on it. The cookie trays inched toward the edge. He tugged again. A tray fell on the ground. Cookies scattered across the grass, and a girl screamed. It was

Melanie. Melanie tried to rescue her cookies, but Frankie was too fast. He scarfed them all down. Bruce grabbed Frankie and put him on his leash.

Heidi and Lucy burst out laughing and slapped each other five.

Then Mrs. Crosby stepped up with

the microphone. She waved a big
white envelope in the air.

"We have a winner!" she said.

Everyone clapped and cheered.

Mrs. Crosby opened the envelope
and pulled out the winning name.

"The winner of this year's cookie
contest is . . ." She squinted at the

name. "Lucy Lancaster!"

"WHAT?" cried Lucy.

The crowd burst into cheers.

Heidi almost fell over. *Not Lucy! How can plain sugar cookies win the contest? What is going on?* she wondered.

"Will Lucy please come forward?" asked Mrs. Crosby.

Heidi was still in shock, but she gave Lucy a great big hug. "Wow," she said. "Congratulations!"

"Thanks, Heidi!" said Lucy. "I can't believe it!"

Neither can I, thought Heidi.

Lucy walked to the judges' table. The judges were standing in front of the table with Mrs. Crosby. They took turns praising Lucy's first-place cookies.

"Simple, yet extraordinary," said Principal Pennypacker.

"A pleasing blend of ingredients," said the food editor.

"Crisp on the outside and tender on the inside," said the mayor. "I *must* have the recipe!"

Mrs. Crosby pinned a beautiful blue ribbon on Lucy's shirt.

Lucy posed with the principal and the mayor. A photographer snapped their picture. Heidi stared in disbelief. Her shoulders slumped. She felt like such a loser. Lucy had stuck with a simple recipe and come out on top.

Heidi had gone overboard and made the mayor gag. Mom, Dad, and Henry walked over and patted Heidi on the back.

Heidi moaned. "You were right," she said.

"You had to find out for yourself," said Dad.

"Boy, did I stink up your recipe," said Heidi.

"You certainly did," said Dad.

"They smelled like gym socks," said Heidi.

"Dog poop," said Henry.

"Moldy cheese," said Mom.

Heidi smiled. "Next year I won't change a thing."

"Hallelujah!" said Dad. Then he rubbed his hands together. "So, who wants to sample some cookies?"

"I do!" said Heidi.

"Me too!" said Mom.

"Let's go!" said Henry.

And then the Heckelbecks tasted the cookies—all of them except for Melanie's because, of course, they were all gone.

Woof!

Check out the next book starring

HEiDi HECKELBECK

HEiDi HECKELBECK in Disguise

HERE'S A SNEAK PEEK!

Heidi's class was making place mats for their Halloween party. They cut out black cats, pumpkins, and full moons from construction paper. Heidi named her cat Creepers. It had an arched back and a frizzy tail.

While working, everyone talked about dressing up for Halloween.

An excerpt from *Heidi Heckelbeck in Disguise*

"I'm going to be a skeleton!" said Stanley Stonewrecker.

"I'm going to be a prima ballerina!" said Lucy Lancaster.

"I'm going to be a mad scientist!" said Bruce Bickerson.

"But that makes no sense," said Melanie Maplethorpe. "You already

ARE a mad scientist!" Melanie was famous for saying mean things. She usually picked on Heidi.

An excerpt from *Heidi Heckelbeck in Disguise*

Bruce glared at Melanie. "You're just a wicked WITCH!" he said.

"That's really funny," Melanie said, "because that's exactly what I'm going to be for Halloween—a WITCH! How did you know?"

"Just a feeling," said Bruce.

"Well, JUST SO EVERYONE KNOWS,

An excerpt from *Heidi Heckelbeck in Disguise*

nobody can copy me," said Melanie. "I want to be the ONLY witch in the class."

Lucy squished Heidi's foot under the desk and whispered, "She IS the only witch in the class!"

Heidi usually laughed when Lucy made a joke, but not this time.

Melanie's NOT the only witch in the class! thought Heidi. *She doesn't know the first thing about REAL witches. She's going to be a stupid storybook witch, and that's what gives real witches a bad name.*

Melanie stopped cutting out her cat and looked at Heidi. Heidi's face had turned bright red. She looked like she might explode at any second.

"What's YOUR problem, weirdo?" asked Melanie.

Heidi wanted to scream a million mean things in Melanie's face, but she felt totally tongue-tied. Heidi made her meanest face ever instead. But Melanie kept right on talking.

"So, Miss Weirdo, have you picked out a Halloween costume?"

"None of your business," said Heidi, trying to sound tough.

"Well, no need to bother," Melanie said. "Be what you are—a total NUT!"

"Melanie Maplethorpe!" said Lucy, with her hands on her hips. "If I looked up 'evil' in the dictionary, I'd find a picture of you."

"Why, thank you!" said Melanie. "That's the nicest thing anyone's said to me all day." Then she flipped her blond hair over her shoulder and began to walk away. "And by the way," she added, turning to Heidi, "as long as we're playing Dictionary, we all know the definition of 'weirdo' is Heidi."